Snow Bunny's Christmas Gift

Rebecca Harry

little bee books

Snow Bunny
lived in the forest with her friends
Mouse, Fox, and Bear.

One snowy morning
just before Christmas,
Snow Bunny knotted the ties
on her little red cape and set
off to find her friends.

Mouse, Bear, and Fox were
all ready for a day of fun
in the snow.
"What shall we do?"
asked Mouse.

"I know," said Snow Bunny.
"Let's go sledding on Honey
Hill. It's the *perfect* place!"

And off they went.

Soon Snow Bunny,
Mouse, Fox, and Bear
were racing down Honey Hill.

Wheee! It was such fun . . . but the
winter wind whipped and howled.

"I'm ch-ch-ch-chilly," said Mouse after a while.
"I want to go home." And off she scampered.

Snow Bunny, Fox, and Bear felt sad.
"What shall we do now?" asked Fox.

"I know," said Snow Bunny.
"Let's go skating on Shining Lake.
It's the *perfect* place!"

And off they went.

Snow Bunny, Fox, and Bear looped
and twirled across the ice.

Whizzzz!

But gray clouds soon covered the winter sun.

"I'm c-c-c-cold," Fox whimpered after a while.
"I want to go home." And off he trotted.

Snow Bunny and Bear
felt very sad.
"What shall we do now?"
asked Bear.

"I know," said Snow Bunny.
"Let's gather pine cones in
Treetop Forest.
It's the *perfect* place!"
But just as they reached
the forest, huge snowflakes
began to fall.

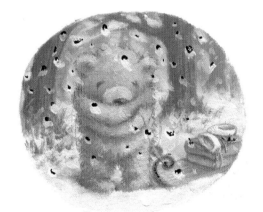

"I'm f-f-f-frozen," Bear
shivered after a while.
"I want to go home."
And off he trudged.

Snow Bunny felt sadder
than ever. "What shall I
do now?" she sighed.
"All my friends have gone.
I'll just have to go home
all by myself."

Night was falling, and
Snow Bunny was nearly home
when suddenly, she stopped.
Something was glistening
in the snow.

It was a bright, silver coin,
sparkling in the moonlight.
"Ooooh!" said Snow Bunny,
and she popped the coin in the pocket
of her cape. "What shall I do now?"

And, all of a sudden, she had a wonderful idea.
"I know the *perfect* place!" she said.

And off she went.

Snow Bunny reached Mr. Badger's
shop just as it was about to close.
"Oh, please, Mr. Badger," said Snow Bunny,
holding up her silver coin, "I just need *one* thing."

"What would you like?"
said Mr. Badger.

"Please may I have one of
those?" Snow Bunny asked,
pointing to a shelf.

Then, clutching her package,
Snow Bunny hurried home
through the dark.

Back in her cozy cottage,
Snow Bunny set to work.
All night long, as the icy
wind blew and the gray
clouds covered the winter
moon and the snow fell,
she knitted and knitted
and knitted . . . until,
finally, *everything*
was ready.

The next day was Christmas
Day, and Snow Bunny set off
through the glittering snow.
First she went to Mouse's
house. "I've brought you
a gift," she said.

Mouse unwrapped her present.
Snow Bunny had knitted her a
little hat with a pom-pom
on top. "Thank you!"
Mouse said.
"Now I won't be chilly!"

Then Snow Bunny went to Fox's house.
"I've brought you a gift," she said.

Fox unwrapped his present. Snow Bunny had knitted him a long,
woolly scarf. "Thank you!" Fox said. "Now I won't be cold!"

Finally, Snow Bunny arrived at Bear's house.
"I've brought you a gift," she said.

Bear unwrapped his present.
Snow Bunny had knitted him
a cozy vest with
a big, shiny button.

"Thank you!" Bear said.
"Now I won't be freezing!" And he gave
Snow Bunny a big bear hug.

Later, when the sun was setting, Snow Bunny
and her friends set off to light the candles
on the Christmas tree.

Snow Bunny wore her cape. Mouse wore her
little hat with the pom-pom on top. Fox wore
his long, woolly scarf. And Bear wore
his cozy vest with the big,
shiny button.

They all had a lovely time.
"But we don't have a gift for you, Snow Bunny,"
said her friends.

Snow Bunny looked at her friends, so warm and snug in
their new clothes, and smiled. "I don't mind one bit,"
said Snow Bunny . . .

"because *friendship* is the *greatest gift* of all.
Merry Christmas, everyone!"

For Jon, with love xxx

R.H.

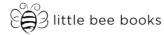 little bee books

An imprint of Bonnier Publishing Group

853 Broadway, New York, New York 10003

Text copyright © 2014 by Nosy Crow Ltd.

Illustrations copyright © 2014 by Rebecca Harry.

This little bee books edition, 2015.

Manufactured in Shenzhen, China 0415

First Edition 2 4 6 8 10 9 7 5 3 1

Library of Congress Control Number: 2015934156

ISBN 978-1-4998-0164-4

www.littlebeebooks.com

www.bonnierpublishing.com